Robert Quackenbush

DANGER IN TIBET

A Miss Mallard Mystery

Pippin Press
New York

For Piet and Margie

Published by Pippin Press, 229 East 85th Street
Gracie Station Box 92
New York, N.Y. 10028

Printed in Spain by Novograph, S.A., Madrid.

10 9 8 7 6 5 4 3 2

Library of Congress Cataloging-in-Publication Data

Quackenbush, Robert M.
    Danger in Tibet.

    Summary: The world-famous ducktective investigates
the disappearance of her nephew, Inspector Willard
Widgeon, during a secret mission in the Himalayas,
and uncovers a dastardly plot that could destroy
Mt. Everest.

    [1. Ducks—Fiction.   2. Mystery and detective
stories]   I. Title.
PZ7.Q16Dan   1989   [Fic]   88-31756
ISBN 0-945912-03-X

LAMA LA, TIBET
JULY 10TH

DEAR AUNTY,

DON'T BELIEVE WHAT YOU HEAR.
IF I AM STOPPED, YOU MUST TAKE OVER.
THE SECRET IS IN THE LOST CITY OF
SAGA HAPI. TRUST NO ONE.

CHEERS,
Willard
WILLARD

Miss Mallard, the world famous ducktective, rode on the back of a yak in the foothills of Mount Everest. She was searching for her nephew, Inspector Willard Widgeon, who vanished while tracking down the thief who stole a million dollars in Swiss gold.

Her concern for Willard and a puzzling note from him brought Miss Mallard to Tibet. She received the note on the very day he was reported missing. She was heading for Lama La, the village where it had been mailed. She was determined to solve the mystery.

When she arrived at Lama La, Miss Mallard found an inn where Willard had taken a room. She questioned the owner of the inn, Nevel Tree Duck, and his housekeeper, Trempe.

"I keep my mind only on my cleaning and not on the guests," said Trempe.

Nevel knew more. He told Miss Mallard that Willard hired a porter named Salum and went climbing up Mount Everest. Willard paid for his room in advance so he could store some of his things while he was away.

"But he never came back," said Nevel. "Salum lost sight of him in a storm."

Miss Mallard asked to see Willard's room. Trempe went back to cleaning and Nevel led the way. As they were going down a narrow hall, Miss Mallard asked if there were any guests who she could question. Nevel said they were all away on mountain climbing expeditions.

Nevel unlocked the door to Willard's room with a master key from the lobby. They went inside and gasped. The room had been ransacked!

"Look!" said Nevel, pointing to an open window.

They ran to the window and looked out. They saw prints in the mud below the window. Miss Mallard looked at the prints and then back in the room. Something bothered her.

She turned to Nevel and said, "Does Saga Hapi mean anything to you?"

"Strange you should ask that now," said Nevel. "It is a haven of peace and beauty that legend says is somewhere on Mount Everest. The waters there are believed to give everlasting youth."

"Hmmm," said Miss Mallard. "Please fetch Salum for me."

When Nevel left, Miss Mallard got busy looking for clues. She saw a gold coin on the floor. She was sure that it had been dropped by the intruder. Next she found a file for Willard's police reports. It was empty!

"So!" thought Miss Mallard. "The intruder was after the reports."

Then Miss Mallard saw a box of chocolates on the table. It was the only thing of Willard's that had not been touched. She examined the box and found a piece of paper hidden under the candy. A map was scribbled on it!

"Just like Willard," thought Miss Mallard. "He left me a clue in the very place he knew I would look. Only I know about his fondness for chocolates."

She studied the map. She was more puzzled than ever. The map showed how to get to Saga Hapi. She wondered what a lost city had to do with a robbery.

Miss Mallard put the clues in her knitting bag. Then she straightened up Willard's room. That done, she went to the lobby and saw that Salum had arrived. Trempe was quacking at him for wearing muddy boots.

"I just cleaned the floor," Trempe was saying. "Take them off!"

Salum humbly removed his boots and came inside. Miss Mallard asked him to take her where he had last seen Willard, but he protested.

Nevel said, "Let me explain why Salum doesn't think you should go. Climbing Mount Everest is very dangerous. And you know what happened to your nephew."

"You're wrong," said Miss Mallard. "I don't know what happened to my nephew. But I intend to find out. Besides, my brisk walks and aerobics have prepared me for mountain climbing."

There was no stopping her. Early the next morning Miss Mallard left with Salum in search of her nephew. Remembering Willard's warning to trust no one, she took along her own compass.

Together they climbed up the mountain. Higher and higher they went. By afternoon they were trudging in snow and ice. Suddenly, they came upon huge footprints!

"Yeti! Yeti!" quacked Salum as he turned and ran back to the village.

Miss Mallard could not stop him. She knew what frightened him away. Yeti was the dreaded word in Tibet for the Abominable Snowduck, a giant creature who was said to roam the mountain. No one had ever seen him, though his prints had been discovered many times by climbers of Mount Everest.

All at once it was snowing. A storm was brewing. Miss Mallard braced herself against the wind and snow and kept on climbing. The snow kept whirling around her. Soon she could not see where she was going. She reached into her knitting bag for her compass and Willard's map to find her way. As she fumbled for the compass she dropped it. It slid and fell into a bottomless ice crevice!

Miss Mallard was very worried. Without a compass, she knew she could never find her way. She kept on climbing, hoping to find shelter from the storm. She tripped and stumbled as she climbed. Finally, she fell into the snow so exhausted that she couldn't get up.

"I must not go to sleep," she kept saying over and over to herself.

The next thing Miss Mallard knew, she was being picked up and carried.

"What's happening?" she muttered.

She looked up through dazed eyes and saw the face of the Abominable Snowduck. He was smiling. The giant creature carried her to the shelter of a cliff and left her there.

As she watched the Abominable Snowduck leave, Miss Mallard thought, "Why didn't I remember to bring a camera?"

She felt safe in the shelter of the cliff. She was aware of warm air coming from around the bend of the cliff. She walked toward the warmth. What did she see?

She saw a splendid city and someone rushing to greet her.

"Willard!" cried Miss Mallard.

"I knew you would come, Aunty," said her nephew. "Welcome to Saga Hapi. Did you bring my box of chocolates?"

"How can you think of chocolates at a time like this, Willard?" said Miss Mallard. "Tell me why you are here."

"Come with me, Aunty," replied Willard. "I'll take you to meet the High Lama. He's the ruler of Saga Hapi. He'll explain everything to you. But first you must refresh yourself with the amazing waters of Saga Hapi."

Miss Mallard drank the water. She felt restored and full of energy at once. They went on their way to see the High Lama.

The meeting took place in a great hall. The kindly ruler told Miss Mallard how a master criminal found an ancient map of Saga Hapi in a book shop in Switzerland. The map gave the criminal the idea for an evil scheme. He trained for mountain climbing and then robbed a bank of a million dollars in gold. When that was done, he set out to buy Saga Hapi. His scheme was to make it into a resort and to bottle the amazing water to sell worldwide.

"He intends to make billions of dollars and rule the world with his power," said the High Lama. "If we don't accept his offer and move out of Saga Hapi in a month, he will blow everything to smithereens."

"Good Heavens!" said Miss Mallard. "Who is this demon?"

"No one has ever seen him, Aunty," said Willard. "He always wears disguises. I was able to trace him to Tibet through the gold coins he spent along the way."

"But how did you get here, Willard?" asked Miss Mallard.

Willard replied, "News of my mission reached Saga Hapi. A messenger gave me a map so I could meet with the High Lama and plan a way to catch the crook. I left a copy of the map for you, Aunty, in the chocolate box. On my way here I got lost in a storm, but I was rescued by the Abominable Snowduck."

"A fine fellow, that Snowduck," said the High Lama.

"He rescued me, too," said Miss Mallard.

She thought about the Abominable Snowduck's tracks that she had seen in the snow. Suddenly, she remembered what had bothered her about Willard's room.

"We must hurry back to the village, Willard," she said. "I know who is behind the dreadful scheme."

"Our guides will lead the way," said the High Lama.

With the help of the guides, Miss Mallard and Willard made a hasty return to the inn. They asked Salum, Nevel, and Trempe to assemble in the lobby.

"Why are we here?" asked Trempe.

Miss Mallard held up the coin from her knitting bag and said, "It is about this piece of gold. It comes from the loot of a million dollar robbery. It was dropped by the robber when he ransacked Willard's room to destroy the police reports. He made it appear as if someone entered the room from the outside by making fake prints in the mud below the opened window. But he forgot to make the muddy prints continue into the room, which proved it was an inside job. Only someone at war against dirt— but not his own dirty work—would have failed to do that. And that someone is…"

Just then, Trempe rushed from the lobby, tripped on Miss Mallard's knitting bag, and went crashing to the floor, sending fake glasses flying.

"Slippery Teal—Switzerland's most wanted crook!" cried Willard. "I should have known! You're under arrest."

"You don't know what you are doing," said Slippery, as he held up his map of Saga Hapi. "I can make you all rich."

Miss Mallard ran over and grabbed the map and threw it into the fire with the copies she and Willard had.

"What have you done!" cried Slippery. "Now no one will ever be able to find Saga Hapi again!"

"I know," said Miss Mallard. "It is safe forever from schemers like you."

In all the excitement, Nevel and Salum were quacking their heads off. Miss Mallard went over to calm them down.

"Don't worry about it," she said. "I didn't expect either of you to know what was going on. But I had to be sure."

After the gold was recovered from Slippery's room and he was taken off to jail, a package came for Miss Mallard. It was a bottle of water from Saga Hapi with a note from the High Lama thanking her for all that she had done.

"How nice!" said Miss Mallard. "I think I'll have a drink right now. The strength I'll receive from this amazing water will help me to do something that should be done before I leave Tibet. It is time the first duck climbed to the top of the world—all the way to the summit of Mount Everest!"

And true to her word, that is exactly what Miss Mallard did.